真美味！我們一起吃！

Yum! Let's Eat!

Thando Maclaren

Illustrated by Jacqueline East

Chinese translation by Sylvia Denham

Mantra Lingua

我是瑪利亞，我的媽媽正在
煮菜汁撈麵。
真美味！我最喜歡吃！

I'm Maria and my mama's
making pasta primavera.

Yum

Yum

Yummy!

My favourite!

我的名字是格貝雅娜，我的家人喜歡吃香辣的辣椒和薄餅。
真美味！我最喜歡吃！

My name's Gabriela. My family loves eating hot, spicy chilli and fajitas.

Yum

Yum

Yummy!

My favourite!

我是卡力，我們去探訪祖父時，
都會吃蒸丸子
和燜辣羊肉。
真美味！我最喜歡吃！

I'm Khaled. We eat couscous and lamb tagine when we visit Grandpa.

Yum

Yum

Yummy!

My favourite!

我是阿格達，我的祖母正在為我和姐姐煮她拿手的波蘭燉肉。真美味！我最喜歡吃！

My name's Agata. My granny is making her special bigos for me and my big sister.

Yum

Yum

Yummy!

My favourite!

我是杜恩，我喜歡吃青豆
米飯和羊肉咖喱。
真美味！我最喜歡吃！

I’m Dwayne and I love eating
rice and peas with goat curry.

Yum
Yum
Yummy!

My favourite!

我的名字是儀敏，我媽媽
正在造粟米炒雞肉。
真美味！我最喜歡吃！

My name's Yi-Min. My mum is making stir fry with chicken and baby corn.

Yum

Yum

Yummy!

My favourite!

食飯時間

我是阿卑巴，我的家人喜歡吃
埃塞俄比亞薄餅和辛辣的烤燉肉。
真美味！我最喜歡吃！

I'm Abeba and my family loves
eating injera with spicy zigni.

Yum
Yum
Yummy!

My favourite!

我的名字是愛子，我正在跟
哥哥姐姐一起吃麵條和壽司。
真美味！我最喜歡吃！

My name's Aiko. I'm eating noodles and sushi with my brother and sister.

Yum
Yum
Yummy!

My favourite!

我是比蒂，我的祖母為爸爸和我造燜扁豆、薄餅及芒果酸乳酪。
真美味！我最喜歡吃！

I'm Priti and my granny makes dhal and roti, with mango lassi for me and daddy.

Yum

Yum

Yummy!

My favourite!

我是查理，我正在與爸爸媽媽一起吃馬鈴薯碎肉批。真美味！我最喜歡吃！

My name's Charlie. I'm having shepherd's pie with Mum and Dad.

Yum

Yum

Yummy!

My favourite!

我是阿仙，我喜歡跟爸爸和哥哥一起吃菜飽及烤肉串。真美味！我最喜歡吃！

I'm Yasin and I love eating kebabs and dolma with Daddy and my big brother.

Yum

Yum

Yummy!

My favourite!

Turkey
Poland
India
Mexico
Jamaica
Japan
Italy
Morocco
Ethiopia
UK
China